W9-ACH-179

7 Days till ice cream

by Bernardo Feliciano
illustrated by Rayanne Vieira

Kane Press
New York

To my beautiful wife Ann and my daughters Nelle and Anjali. Together, we solve the puzzles we find in the world. Also, to the real Jerron, Cha, and JJ. And Eir, the Zany Ice Cream Man.
—B.A.F.

To Mom and Israel. Thank you for all the support you give me.
—R.V.

Library of Congress Cataloging-in-Publication Data
Names: Feliciano, Bernardo, author. | Vieira, Rayanne, illustrator.
Title: 7 days till ice cream / by Bernardo Feliciano ; illustrated by Rayanne Vieira.
Other titles: Seven days till ice cream | 7 days until ice cream
Description: New York : Kane Press, [2020] | Series: Makers make it work |
Summary: Cha, Jerron, and A.J. use what they learned at computer coding camp to alter the ice cream truck's route so it passes by them on Sunday.
Identifiers: LCCN 2019010466 (print) | LCCN 2019013922 (ebook) |
ISBN 9781635922721 (ebook) | ISBN 9781635922714 (pbk) | ISBN 9781635922707 (reinforced library binding)
Subjects: | CYAC: Ice cream trucks—Fiction. | Problem solving—Fiction. | Computer programming—Fiction.
Classification: LCC PZ7.1.F447 (ebook) | LCC PZ7.1.F447 Aah 2020 (print) |
DDC [E]—dc23
LC record available at https://lccn.loc.gov/2019010466

10 9 8 7 6 5 4 3 2 1

Kane Press

An imprint of Boyds Mills & Kane, a division of Astra Publishing House

www.kanepress.com

Printed in the United States of America

"It's coming!" Jerron leaned forward and looked down the street. The ice cream truck was just a block away.

"I haven't had ice cream in ages," A.J. said.

"Since last Sunday," Cha added.

Every Sunday, Jerron's uncle bought them ice cream. His parents almost never let them get any. On Sundays, it was a special treat.

"Wait, wha—?" Jerron groaned.

Before the ice cream truck reached them, it turned right. It drove off down another street.

Cha threw her baseball hat to the ground. "Not again!" she said.

Cha, A.J., and Jerron were waiting at Jerron's uncle's house. Sometimes Uncle Bernie's house was on the ice cream truck's route on Sunday.

And sometimes . . . it wasn't.

"I don't get it," said A.J. "The ice cream guy was headed this way!"

"Maybe something made him turn," Cha said.

Jerron nodded. "It's weird, but there must be some logic to it. I'll bet we can figure it out."

"By Sunday," A.J. said. Sunday was their next chance for ice cream from Uncle Bernie. "Right? Seven days. Seven days till ice cream. Deal?"

Jerron put out his hand. Cha covered it with her hand. A.J. placed his on top. "Deal," they agreed.

The next day, they staked out the street. A.J. sat on Uncle Bernie's stoop. Cha waited two blocks away. Jerron stood on the corner where the ice cream man had turned.

Right at three o'clock, Jerron heard the music. The truck was on its way! It got to the corner. Would it go straight?

It turned right . . . again!

Why?

Jerron looked around. The street seemed fine. No potholes. No big puddles. Just Granny Lou-Lou's cat Midnight sleeping in the sun.

Jerron raced down the street. Cha and A.J. ran toward him. "Hey!" he yelled. "I'll bet the ice cream dude doesn't like black cats!"

"Black cats?" said Cha.

"Maybe he thinks a black cat is bad luck—" said Jerron.

"So he turns right when he sees it," Cha finished for him.

"If that's true, we can test this," A.J. said. "It's like . . . a computer program."

Cha nodded. "We'll crack his code!"

The three friends had gone to camp together earlier that summer. They learned to code and program video games and made their computers do cool and funny things.

Coding is the process of writing instructions for a computer in a way—or code—that it understands. A computer reads the code and follows the coder's instructions.

They made a plan for the next day. They planned for everything, except—

A.J. frowned. "Where will we get black cats?"

They all cried at once, "I have an idea!"

A computer program is a list of instructions that a computer follows one at a time. The computer starts at the beginning of the list, reads the instruction, and does what it says. Then the computer reads the next instruction and does what it says. It keeps doing this until it reaches the end of the list.

Tuesday morning, A.J. and Cha arrived with their supplies—poster board and black markers.

"Where's Jerron?" asked Cha.

"There he is," A.J. said.

Jerron was holding a can of tuna.
Behind him was a whole bunch of cats!
Jerron shrugged. "Midnight likes tuna."

“Right,” said Cha. “Let’s set up our test.”

“Will a black cat make the ice cream dude turn right?” said Jerron.

“But don’t we want the ice cream dude to go straight?” asked A.J.

“First, we’ll see what he does if he sees a black cat,” Cha said. “Next, we’ll test for when the condition is false.”

"False? You mean when he checks for a black cat and doesn't see one?" asked A.J.

"Yup," Cha said. "That's the only way to know he's turning right for the cat, not something else."

A *condition* in programming is something that must be true in order for something to happen. **If** the condition is true, **then** the computer will perform a particular instruction *before* it continues to follow the rest of the program. If the condition is false, the program goes on to the next instruction in the program without performing the special instruction.

"Sunday is five days away. We have plenty of time to test." Jerron rubbed his hands together. "I can taste that ice cream now!"

At three o'clock, the friends put the can of tuna on Granny Lou-Lou's corner. Midnight went to eat it. The ice cream man saw her, and . . .

"He turned right!"

"But now he's gone. We can't test for when he doesn't see the cat," said A.J. "Hmmmm. Tomorrow let's try this."

He showed Jerron and Cha a drawing.

On Wednesday, the three friends set up on street corners according to A.J.'s plan.

Jerron kept the cats out of sight. The truck went straight toward Uncle Bernie's house.

Meanwhile, A.J. and Cha paraded with their signs at the corner. When the truck got to them, it turned right!

"Yes! We solved it!" Jerron said. "**If** the ice cream man sees black cats, **then** he goes right. If he doesn't, he goes straight. Keep the cats away on Sunday, and I'm sure he'll go by Uncle Bernie's."

"If we want, we can get him to come back!" Cha grinned. She drew on A.J.'s plan.

"This really is like coding a computer," said A.J., "except it's the ice cream man!"

The next day, the driver circled the block. "Yeah!" Cha cheered. But then something unexpected happened.

The ice cream driver turned left!

"Why did he turn left?" Jerron groaned.

Was it the ladder? Thirteen blackbirds? Kids stepping on sidewalk cracks? Spilled salt packets? The calico cat? They had so many conditions to test. And only two days to do it.

Then on Friday it rained.

"OK," said Cha, with her hands on her hips. "We only have tomorrow to figure out why he turned left. We have to make a plan."

"First, let's make our sketch bigger," suggested Jerron, "with more streets."

"Huh?" A.J. and Cha said at the same time.

Jerron explained, “More streets means more corners . . .”

“And more corners means we can do more tests!” finished A.J.

After making a map of the whole neighborhood, Cha said, “Time to plan.”

By Saturday morning, the map looked like this.

First, the friends tested for all conditions set to false by making sure the first corner was completely clear. Then they tested conditions one by one. This went on all day until . . .

"Ladders! Ladders make him turn left!"

They were ready for Sunday—and ice cream!

On Sunday afternoon, Uncle Bernie pulled into his driveway and said, “Sorry, kids. Looks like no ice cream today. There’s road construction all over the neighborhood.”

Jerron grinned. “Don’t worry, Uncle Bernie,” he said. “We’ve got this.”

Jerron, A.J., and Cha sprang into action. With a black cat at First Avenue . . .

a ladder at
School Street . . .

no cats or ladders
until Fourth . . .

. . . and with one final ladder on Day Street, the friends guided the ice cream truck to Uncle Bernie's door.

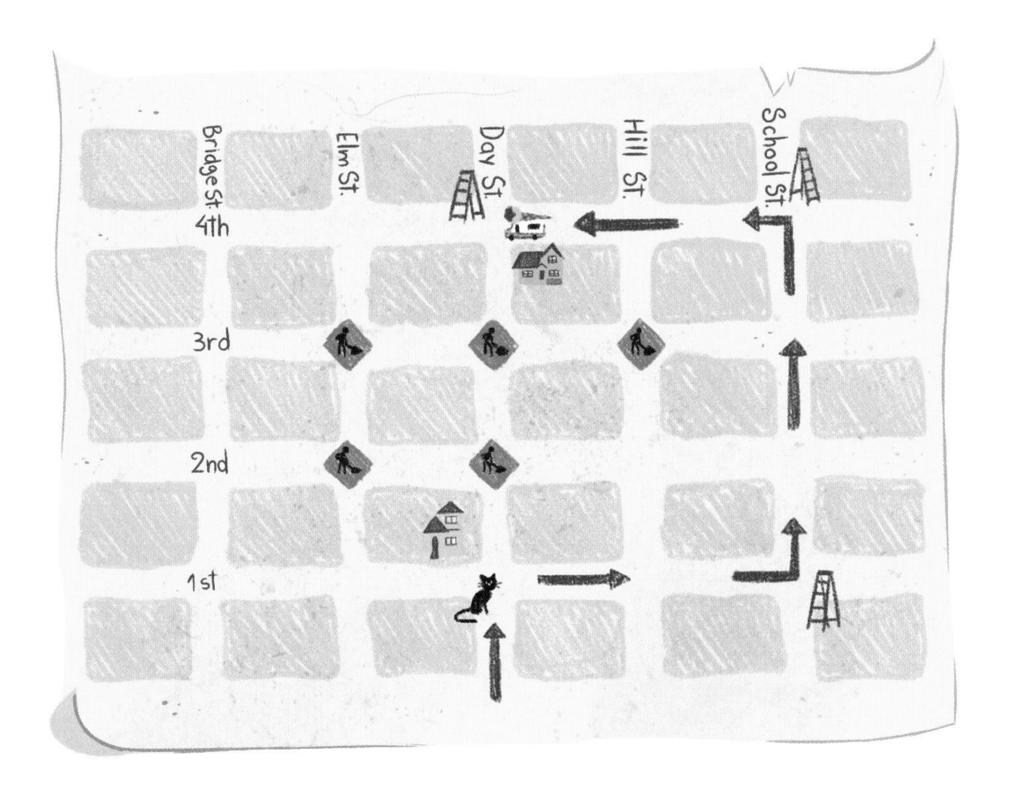

There are actually (at least) two codes here! The kids code the ice cream man—by hiding *or* showing black cats and ladders on corners—to guide him around the neighborhood. But they have to use the code in the ice cream man's head to do this. The funny rules the ice cream man follows are a code, too. Who knows how they got there?

Jerron gave A.J. and Cha fist bumps. "And that," he said, "is how you code the ice cream dude."

Uncle Bernie bought them all ice cream. He even treated the ice cream man to a cone.

"You earned it," he said, "after what these kids put you through."

"Are you kidding?" said the ice cream man. "I sold more ice cream this week than I have all summer!"

There are many ways to solve a coding problem. Jerron, Cha, and A.J. found one solution. How would *you* program the ice cream truck?

Learn Like a Maker

Why did the ice cream truck driver keep turning right? Jerron, Cha, and A.J. used logic to figure out how to get him to come their way. They found out that coding the ice cream man was kind of like coding a computer!

Look Back

- How does the picture on page 19 show the results of Jerron, Cha, and A.J.'s plan?
- Reread pages 28 and 29. Draw a map to show a different way to get the ice cream truck to Uncle Bernie's house.

Try This!

Write a Code

Use coding logic to get a friend from one point to another. All you need is paper in three different colors. Arrange the papers on the ground to guide your friends. If they follow the code, then they will reach the red paper at the end.

Code:

- Begin at "Start." Walk until you reach a colored paper on the ground.
- If the paper is yellow, turn right.
- If the paper is blue, turn left.
- If the paper is red, stop.

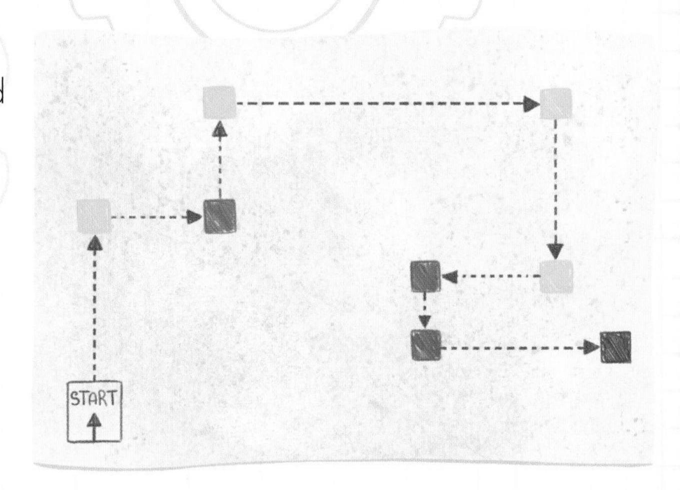

What other codes can you come up with?